PUFFIN BOOKS

RAGDOLLY ANNA'S CIRCUS

Ragdolly Anna lives with the Little Dressmaker, Dummy and the White Cat in a flat on the fifth floor. She's a very special doll and she just can't help having the most exciting adventures!

This time, she helps the White Cat celebrate his birthday, gets chicken-pox and is kidnapped by a fox!

Jean Kenward is married, with six grandchildren. She writes poetry, songs and stories for BBC Schools programmes and her work for both adults and children has been published in various collections and anthologies. You can find more of Ragdolly Anna's adventures in *Ragdolly Anna* and *Three Cheers for Ragdolly Anna*, both in Young Puffin.

Other books by Jean Kenward

RAGDOLLY ANNA
THREE CHEERS FOR RAGDOLLY ANNA

Jean Kenward

*

RAGDOLLY ANNA'S CIRCUS

Illustrated by Sally Holmes

Puffin Books

Puffin Books, Penguin Books Ltd, Harmondsworth, Middlesex, England
Viking Penguin Inc., 40 West 23rd Street, New York, New York 10010, U.S.A.
Penguin Books Australia Ltd, Ringwood, Victoria, Australia
Penguin Books Canada Ltd, 2801 John Street, Markham, Ontario, Canada L3R 1B4
Penguin Books (N.Z.) Ltd, 182–190 Wairau Road, Auckland 10, New Zealand

First published 1987

Made and printed in Great Britain by
Richard Clay Ltd, Bungay, Suffolk

Typeset in Baskerville

Contents

*

Ragdolly Anna's Circus

*

The White Cat liked to give Ragdolly Anna what he called Reading Instruction every day. She learned well, and was soon able to recognize a great many short words like 'and' or 'but'; and sometimes 'hat' or 'roses'. As she struggled on, the words got longer and longer.

'You must be able to spell, as well as to read,' commented the White Cat. 'Now take down these . . . mmmmiew . . . RHODODENDRON (a shrub) . . . MADAGASCAR (a country) . . . PNEUMONIA . . . miew . . . (an illness).'

They were terribly difficult.

'And when you are out shopping with *her*,' he went on, 'be sure to study all the posters. They convey interesting and useful information. I shall expect a poster-reading *every day*.'

Ragdolly Anna looked at several posters while the Little Dressmaker was buying things, and told the White Cat exactly what they had said:

'"A meeting of the W.I. 4.30 Friday. Tea."

"Rummage Sale at the Scout Hut. Entrance 4p."

"Antique Market. All are Welcome."

"Flower Show at Memorial Hall. ONIONS."'

Then, one day she came upon a more unusual one. It had a picture of a man in a funny hat, juggling with plates, and of someone jumping through a hoop on horseback.

'What an extraordinary thing to do,' thought Ragdolly Anna. Underneath the picture, in large yellow letters, she read 'CIRCUS'.

'What's a circus?' she asked the White Cat, as soon as they had got home.

'A form of entertainment – entertainment for humans. Amusement for the Ignorant,' he explained. 'I don't intend to go. Such idiocy! Clowns, too . . . Ridiculous!'

'The tickets are very expensive,' said the Little Dressmaker gently. 'I don't think we can manage an outing this week. But I believe they are putting up the Big Tent in the bit of waste land next to the allotments. We could go and watch.'

And as soon as she had finished her sewing, they went.

'We're going to see them getting the circus ready,' Ragdolly Anna told Dummy in a whisper. 'I'll tell you about it, when we come back.'

Dummy was only half dressed that day: she was wearing part of a fancy-dress costume, and was preparing to be 'Queen of the Night'. Her short, dark bodice was covered in stars, and there was a moon on her skirt. Ragdolly Anna thought she looked lovely. But then, she always did – no matter what she had on.

They set off early that afternoon, waving goodbye, and soon began to hear sounds of movement and excitement.

'This way, Toby, UP she goes!' called someone.

'Where's my hammer?' shouted somebody else . . . and 'Take them horses their oats, Johnny, or they won't jump anything more 'n a caterpillar.'

The circus tent was enormous. Ragdolly Anna and the Little Dressmaker peeped in at the doorway. Inside, a person was practising on a tightrope, high, high up above their heads. Ragdolly Anna caught her breath . . . and the Little Dressmaker had to look the other way, she was so afraid there might be an accident.

' 'E won't fall,' joked a voice behind her, 'and it won't matter if 'e do. There's a net underneath. See it? No one gets 'urt in a net.'

'I suppose not,' agreed the Little Dressmaker, but she continued to feel a trifle faint. They moved on. Round the back was a different sort of tent altogether – a sound of neighing came from it, a pawing of the ground, and now and then a snort. It was a canvas stable for the circus horses. They were having their beautiful silky tails washed and plaited, and their flowing manes combed and decorated with coloured ribbons – green, blue, yellow, red, purple and silver. Such a sight . . . 'Oh!' 'Ah!' They watched them for a long time, and were just turning to go when they heard a strange noise.

What could it be?

It sounded like a giant, yawning. But it couldn't be that, for there were no giants in the circus. 'HEE – HAW!'

'I know!' burst out the Little Dressmaker suddenly. 'It's a donkey!'

And so it was.

Tied up to a bit of fencing was a real donkey with a black mark running down his back, as if he had been made in two parts and stuck together. He seemed to be miserable about something, and they tried hard to find out what

it might be. But it was not until the Little Dress-maker had walked off a few steps to look for some thistles for him that Ragdolly Anna realized he was speaking to her.

'Her-low!'

'I didn't know donkeys could talk,' she gasped, stepping backwards quickly.

'Ah,' brayed Mr Donkey, 'that's because you're turning into a human, I dare say. Such a pity. Of course donkeys can talk. Tell me something that doesn't, that's all!'

'There's leaves . . . and stars . . . and . . . and minnows . . .' suggested Ragdolly Anna.

'They *all* talk. Why, you've only got to

listen. Keep your ears open, and *listen*. Stars, now,' he went on dreamily. 'They twinkle. Surely you know the rhyme "Twinkle twinkle, little star"? That's what it's about. They make a great noise, twinkling, they do.'

'Oh,' said Ragdolly Anna.

'Then leaves. It *was* leaves you said, wasn't it? Every leaf's got a different voice. There's no getting away from leaves – they're never silent. Tell me a leaf that's silent, then, tell me THAT,' cried Mr Donkey, triumphantly. 'Even a cabbage can speak! Haven't you heard of Bubble and Squeak? As to minnows . . . of *course* they talk.'

He came closer, and leaned towards her.

(I hope he's not going to fall over, thought Ragdolly Anna. He seems so very tired.)

'You see my ears? You notice how large they are?'

'They certainly *are* rather large,' ventured Ragdolly Anna. 'I didn't like to stare.'

'Why not? *All* the best animals have large ears,' he went on huffily. 'Yours aren't up to much, I must say. They hardly show at all. Well. I hear the conversation of minnows frequently. FREQUENTLY!' he repeated loudly.

Then he sighed. His head drooped, suddenly,

and a tear ran down his nose and burst on Ragdolly Anna's foot.

'What's the matter?'

'I'll tell you,' sniffed Mr Donkey gloomily, 'if you'll promise not to laugh. No laughter, mind. No giggles. I can't stand it.'

Ragdolly Anna promised.

Mr Donkey fidgeted a little, and cleared his throat.

'It's my tail,' he whispered hoarsely.

'Your tail? What's wrong with it?'

'They don't *comb* it. They don't *brush* it out. I *never* get ribbons . . . not even on Gala Night. And after all, I *am* part of the circus. It's my job to cart the forage.'

'Porridge?'

'Not porridge, stupid! Forage. But without ribbons. It makes me feel low . . . eeeeawaw-awaw . . . *very* low.'

Ragdolly Anna looked at his tail. It hung rather limply, and certainly it wouldn't have been easy to brush it out or comb it, for it resembled nothing so much as a length of washing line.

'It's got a lovely tuft on the end,' she said encouragingly. 'Lovely!'

'But *no ribbon*,' repeated Mr Donkey. He began to sniff again. 'So thoughtless. So unfair! Mean . . .'

The Little Dressmaker came up at that moment with a bunch of thistles, and Ragdolly Anna flinched as he took a great mouthful and began to crunch. Perhaps he had learned how not to hurt his tongue?

'When's Gala Night?' she whispered.

'It'll be Saturday,' mumbled Mr Donkey, swallowing a specially prickly prickle. 'And after that, we'll be gone. London . . . Manchester . . . Liverpool . . . the Great Beyond. Some with ribbons. Some without. Ooooooo – hooooooo! Eeeeeee . . . aw!'

The Little Dressmaker was beginning to fidget. She had work to do, she told Ragdolly Anna, and they must hurry to be back home in the flat five floors up before dusk. They left Mr Donkey leaning against the fence, swishing his tail miserably from side to side.

'I wish I had a piece of ribbon,' panted Ragdolly Anna. She usually had to run to keep up with the Little Dressmaker, because her legs weren't very long. She was almost too breathless to speak.

'Ribbon? I don't know what you want it for' (they crossed the road carefully at this point), 'but there's that box which had chocolates in. That's got a big scarlet bow. Would that do? If we could unfasten it? It might be difficult. We'll have to see.'

Ragdolly Anna clapped her hands. 'It would do *perfectly*,' she nodded; and gave a skip.

When she had taken off her coat and lit the gas under the kettle, the Little Dressmaker helped her to find the box, and untie the ribbon, and iron it.

'What's it for?' she asked.

'A secret!' answered Ragdolly Anna. 'Everyone has secrets . . .'

Saturday came at last, and Ragdolly Anna was all ready to go out.

'May I venture to enquire if you have been invited anywhere?' queried the White Cat, sauntering round the door. 'I notice you have an outdoor appearance. I am quick to pick up such things. Mind the traffic! Take a clean handkerchief. Remember your manners. Thank them for having you. And look where you're going. You are, if I might say so, Prone to Accident. Be careful.'

'He means you sometimes get into difficulties, lovey, that's all,' explained the Little Dressmaker. 'But don't be too long. Saturday's a busy day – the streets'll be crowded. Not more than half an hour, at any rate.'

Ragdolly Anna promised she would run all

the way to *Somewhere* and all the way back again. She had folded the ribbon carefully, and wrapped it in a bit of tissue paper to keep it clean.

It seemed a great distance to the circus tents. It always seemed further when she was on her own. She darted up this road, and down that, keeping to the pavements and waiting for a Green Man to tell her when she might cross. She was relieved to see Professor Purrkins crouching drowsily in a bus shelter. She waved, and he twitched, and squinted.

'Hullowwwww? Howwwww are you?' he mewed. 'Going there and back again, are you? Everybody does it. From here to there, you could say; and after that – from there to here. It keeps them busy. Of course, it would be *much* wiser to stay in the same place, and purr. As I do. But we cannot all be wise. You going now? Goodbye, then . . . goodbye . . . remember me to the White Cat . . .'

Mr Donkey was still leaning against the fence behind the stables, almost exactly as they had left him.

'Shut your eyes!' called Ragdolly Anna, as she neared him. 'Don't open them till I say!' She unfolded the tissue paper, and shook out the ribbon. It looked smooth and strong, and was wider than she had remembered. It was the most beautiful shade of red. As red as a holly berry.

'Careful, now! you're doing something to my tail!' grunted Mr Donkey suspiciously. 'It's a trick. It tickles . . . I'm going to look . . .'

He opened his eyes . . . and turned his head.

Wow! A bow! A splendid, big, bright, rather magnificent ribbon was tied on to his tail, just above the tuft. 'EE−AW!' It *was* a surprise!

'I never would have guessed,' he admitted, 'but when I heard the tissue paper crinkling I knew that Something must be Up. "That's not thistles," I said to myself. "That's tissue paper." The question is, what's inside? You never know. It might have been Pins and Needles. Such things do happen.'

'It's to wear on Gala Night,' explained Ragdolly Anna. 'That's this very evening, isn't it? You'll be as smart as the rest of them, now!'

'I shall wear it,' announced Mr Donkey, drawing himself up proudly, 'I shall wear it *every* night. Every night is Gala Night, when you've got a ribbon. We'll be travelling on, tomorrow. London . . . Manchester . . . Birmingham . . . Moreton-in-the-Marsh . . . the Great Unknown. Look out of the window. You may get a treat. You may see me.'

Ragdolly Anna had already turned for home. 'Goodbye!' she called. 'I shall look out for you in the morning!'

In twelve minutes, she was safely back home.

After breakfast the following day, they all made themselves comfortable by the window, for it was common knowledge that the circus would pass that way as it went off to its new destination. They could hear the great vans approaching . . . there was the juggler with his plates . . . the acrobats . . . the lady on the first of the splendid white horses . . . a group of clowns turning somersaults (which made the White Cat put on a very disdainful expression) . . . a fortune-teller . . . a man who played the tambourine. And in the middle of everything, Mr Donkey, with a long dark line down his back as if he had been stuck together, a truck full of forage, and a fine, scarlet ribbon tied in a great bow on the end of his tail.

Ragdolly Anna clapped so loudly that he heard her, and rolled an eye in her direction. He certainly had the most enormous ears. But the ribbon suited him. He didn't look sad any more.

'E E E-aw!' he called, proudly, as he passed by.

I don't think that Dummy had ever heard

such a sound before. She tottered a little, and had to lean against the sill to stop herself falling. A new word had floated into her empty old nut of a head. The White Cat believed he heard her whisper it. 'Yessss,' he murmured, folding his paws under himself tidily. 'At least, you may be sure that she *thought* she said it: "Circus!" And why not?'

Ragdolly Anna
Becomes a Snowperson

*

Ragdolly Anna lay in bed, wondering. It was morning. But what a *strange* morning! There was a curious lightness everywhere.

She climbed out of her covers, and went to look.

'It's snowed in the night,' the Little Dressmaker told her, pouring out a hot cup of tea. 'I *thought* we were in for a fall. Fancy the milkman having to go out so early! I can hear him, now. His hands *must* be cold. Run and ask him if he'd like a warm drink, Ragdolly Anna, before he goes any further.'

Ragdolly Anna hurried out of the door, and downstairs. She liked the milkman, and didn't want to miss him. He was just putting the bottles on the steps when she got there, and said he would be very pleased to have a drink. He stood by the door, stamping the snow off his boots and trying not to make a mess, and the Little Dressmaker brought down a steaming mug.

'Ah! That's better, that is!' breathed the milkman gratefully. He blew on his hands. Ragdolly Anna noticed that he was wearing mittens.

'You want to come and help me?' he asked her. 'You want to be a Delivery Girl? You couldn't manage the bottles ... they're too heavy ... but the yogs, now. You could carry them. Save me a lot of trouble, that would.'

Ragdolly Anna was pleased. She liked the idea of a ride in the milkman's van.

'You'd better wrap up warm,' advised the Little Dressmaker, and she hurried back upstairs and returned with wraps and scarves, gloves and shawls, and a pair of good felt boots she had made with plastic sewn on the outside to keep them dry.

'There! Now you'll be all right! Don't be too long,' she said. 'Just this road, and the next. And then come back.'

Ragdolly Anna set off with the milkman. She sat in the front of the van, and every time they stopped at a house which wanted yoghurt as well as milk, she got down and hurried up the path with a yoghurt carton. So there were two rows of footprints: one small, and one large.

Before long, it started snowing again. Some of the houses had snowmen in their gardens already. Ragdolly Anna liked to stop and look at them.

There was one snowman with a scarf, and a cap with a feather in it. He wore three stone buttons down his front, and had a pipe in his mouth. As she waited for the milkman to come back with some empty bottles, she felt sure the snowman had said something. At least, *nearly* sure. He had moved his lips, just a little . . .

'Nice wevver for Eskimos!' he had whispered. Or had he?

'Now!' muttered the milkman. 'Here's a pretty

to-do! I've run out of my gold tops. I'll have to nip back to the Dairy, and collect some more. You coming with me, Ragdolly Anna? Or are you going to stay here? I shan't be long.'

'I'll stay here,' replied Ragdolly Anna. 'With the snowman,' she added.

'A snowman'll be company,' agreed the milkman. 'Bye for now, then. Don't get lost!'

He drove off, rattling the empty bottles as he went.

It didn't stop snowing. Soon, even the marks of tyres were covered up with a new whiteness.

'Come to join me?' whispered the snowman. 'There'll be two, then, won't there? Twice one is two!' He heaved a little, hunching his shoulders, and there was a soft slither of snow . . .

It was then that Ragdolly Anna heard a noise of children coming nearer, on their way to school. They were snowballing each other, and some of the boys were rolling an enormous ball that would easily become a snowman if it had a smaller one on top, for a head. They were shouting and laughing together.

Ragdolly Anna trembled. 'I'd better keep still – *quite* still,' she thought. 'Or I might get into difficulties.'

And as the children clustered round her, she stiffened, and was careful not to move at all. Even breathing was dangerous.

At first, they admired the big snowman, with his pipe and buttons.

'And there's another here – a little 'un!' cried one boy. 'Needs building up a bit! Look at that hat!'

He arranged a handful of snow on top of Ragdolly Anna's hat, and pressed it down.

'Good, ain't it?' he cried out to the others. 'Looks almost real!'

'I *am* real,' whispered Ragdolly Anna, under her breath. 'Oh dear! They're turning me into a snowperson! Whatever will happen next?'

'Tell you what,' chuckled another boy. 'It ain't very big. Let's take it to school, this one! I got a plastic bag that'll make a sledge. We can pull it. They'll think there's an extra person in the class. It'll be a fine trick!'

'Yes! Let's do that!' cried several children. And before she had time to say 'No!', even if she had dared, Ragdolly Anna was lifted on to a big plastic bag, and dragged off, slithering.

'Here we go!'

By this time, she was covered with a new whiteness, and began to feel like a snowperson as well as look like one.

As they swirled into the school gates, she was frozen stiff.

'Let's wait until Assembly, and then bring

her in,' decided the biggest boy. 'She'll melt, if we take her too soon.'

They ran off, leaving their plastic sledge just outside the cloakroom. In a moment or two, a bell rang, and a great rush of children began to collect in the Assembly Hall. Ragdolly Anna was carried along with them. The doors swung behind her. She was inside.

How hot it was! And what a lot of pushing and shoving, shouting and calling!

'What you got there, George? A snowman?'

'What's that snowman doing in here, then?'

'We got a new pupil?'

'That's not a snowman – that's a snow lady!'

To Ragdolly Anna's relief, the snow was beginning to melt. A pool gathered round her.

'Where's all this water coming from?'

'Boiler's sprung a leak!'

'That's not a snow lady. That's a dolly!'

The piano began to play the first hymn.

'Now's my chance!' thought Ragdolly Anna. Waiting until all the children were singing at once, with their eyes on their song sheets, she made a quick dart along the row . . . up this one, and down that . . . through the door into the corridor . . . further and further, as fast as she could run.

But the big door out into the grounds was locked.

'I can't get out!' wept Ragdolly Anna. 'I can't open it! I'm not big enough!'

'Not BIG enough?' mewed a familiar voice. She turned round. '*Some* people,' it went on, 'get themselves into difficulties. What you might call an Unfortunate Predicament. You want help?'

It was the White Cat.

'Oh, oh, I am glad to see you,' breathed Ragdolly Anna. She sniffed. Perhaps things weren't going to be so bad after all. 'What are you doing here?'

'Inspecting the milk supplies, of course,' mewed the White Cat. 'Some of the children don't finish their bottles. *Such* a waste. *I* finish it, for them. I tip it over . . . and lap it up . . . and that's that. A public duty. What *you* are doing might be a more important question!'

'I was helping . . . helping the milkman . . .' explained Ragdolly Anna. 'But he had to go off to the Dairy and get some more milk. I turned into a snowperson.'

'A snowperson?'

'They *thought* I was a snowperson. I nearly froze. And then, I nearly melted.'

'Very silly indeed,' criticized the White Cat. 'Anyone could see that you are nearly human. Mind you, anyone who could see *anything*. But some can't. Follow me. I'll let you out. I know the way!'

With a leap, he made a passage through the kitchen window . . . and there was the milkman already at the door, with a crate full of bottles for school delivery.

'So *there* you are, Ragdolly Anna!' he cried. 'What a relief! I was getting worried. Thought you'd been swept up with the snow, somewhere. You're just in time for a lift home. I've finished my round, now, and I'll be passing your flat on my way back to the works.'

Ragdolly Anna sighed happily. 'I *was* nearly swept up with the snow,' she told him. 'I nearly froze. I nearly melted.'

They passed the snowman with a pipe in his mouth on their journey; and Ragdolly Anna gave a secret wave.

'You *have* been a long time!' said the Little Dressmaker, as she came to the door. 'Where *did* you go? Your hat is soaking wet!'

'I've been a snowperson,' explained Ragdolly Anna. 'I've had adventures. The White Cat rescued me.'

'You must change at once, and put on some dry clothes,' worried the Little Dressmaker. 'And we'll have some buttered toast. It'll warm you up. Dummy, too! A snowperson! I never heard of such a thing! What next!'

When they had finished their buttered toast, she filled a tiny hot-water bottle for Ragdolly

Anna, and put her in bed with it for a rest, in case she had caught a chill.

Ragdolly Anna lay with her eyes wide open, looking out. It was still snowing. Large, feathery flakes drifted down . . . down . . . down . . .

She noticed that Dummy had a fleck of butter on her chin.

She had always been fond of buttered toast, though no one ever saw her eating it. Her sticky mouth was puckered into an almost-smile.

Ragdolly Anna
Has Chicken-pox

*

Everybody wakes up in the morning. Some
people wake quickly, and jump out of bed as if
they were in a tremendous hurry, and hungry
for breakfast. Other people wake slowly. They
turn over, drowsily, and may even go to sleep
again after the alarm has gone off. When they *do*
get up at last, they have to sit on the edge of the
bed for a minute or two, and remember who
they are.

The Little Dressmaker was never really quite
herself until she had sipped a cup of tea. She
would stand by the window in her old dressing-
gown, drinking, watching the postman and the
newspaper boy far below, and wondering if there
would be any letters for the flat on the fifth
floor. Sometimes there were; but not often. She
always took her tea from a cup with a marigold
painted on it, for that was a nice way to begin

the day. She would have liked a marigold teapot, too; but teapots were expensive.

Ragdolly Anna woke slowly. She enjoyed the few moments best just before she opened her eyes – when she had *almost* remembered who she was, but not quite. Then, little by little, the room became real. There were the curtains . . . drawn back a bit, where the Little Dressmaker was peeping out . . . there was the White Cat, twining himself round her legs, mewing for a saucer of milk; and there was Dummy.

It was Ragdolly Anna's belief that Dummy never went to sleep at all. Yet she always seemed fresh, and cheerful, with her almost-smile. She *nearly* said 'Good Morning', but not quite.

Ragdolly Anna had learnt to dress herself by now. She could do up her buttons without help, and brush her own hair. She could even manage knots and bows, but they were difficult and needed a lot of concentration.

The White Cat would watch, critically.

'What do you want all those clothes for?' he asked, one March morning, wrinkling his nose. 'Waste of effort, if you ask me.'

'To keep me warm, of course,' Ragdolly Anna replied. She fastened her shawl, and went to the mirror to arrange her hat.

She looked rather odd. She seemed to be

walking in rather a wobbly way, and she felt a bit sick.

The White Cat stared.

'You *DO* look peculiar,' he mewed. The dark pupils of his eyes grew round and large, and then shrank until they were as tiny as pins.

Strangely, the face in the mirror that blinked back at Ragdolly Anna appeared to be covered with spots. There were spots on her cheeks, and her chin, and her forehead . . . and even on her arms. Lifting her petticoat, she noticed that there were spots on her legs, too.

'And on the end of your nose!' commented the White Cat, with interest. 'If you *will* try to be human – that's what happens. You've got measles, I wouldn't wonder. Or scarlet fever. Or worse. Ask *her*. *She*'ll tell you.'

The Little Dressmaker took one glance at Ragdolly Anna, and bundled her back to bed.

Then she got out her Medical Dictionary, and looked up SPOTS.

There were lots of different kinds of spots. Big ones, and small ones, and ones that hurt, and ones that didn't hurt, and ones that itched, and ones that looked as if they had come to stay for ever, but which were likely to vanish in an hour or two. When she had taken Ragdolly Anna's temperature, and put a hand on her

forehead to feel how hot it was, the Little Dress-maker gave a sigh of relief.

'It's only chicken-pox,' she decided. 'Nothing worse. That's a mercy, isn't it? You'll soon be over it, but a few days in bed won't do any harm.'

'Chicken-pox?' drawled the White Cat, washing the end of his tail. 'No cat would go in for that sort of thing. Rather common, don't you think?'

The Little Dressmaker didn't answer. She was

busy making a breakfast tray for Ragdolly Anna.

But Ragdolly Anna didn't feel like breakfast.

She grew hotter and hotter, and redder and redder. The spots pricked. They were like stinging nettles.

The White Cat dozed on the eiderdown. Every now and then he opened one eye.

'You'll probably explode, soon,' he said comfortingly. 'Then you'll feel better. Force of combustion, you understand. That's what we call it – we scientists.'

'Combustion means burning,' explained the Little Dressmaker in a whisper '. . . because you're feverish. Don't take any notice. He's only teasing. What you really need is a fan, to cool you down. But we haven't got one. And I can't go to the shops, and leave you alone here. It's very vexing. What shall we do?'

'Use your wits,' advised the White Cat. 'Make one. Go on. It's easy.'

'What with?' The Little Dressmaker was puzzled.

The White Cat arched his back. 'You might imagine,' he said to no one in particular, 'that a grown-up person would know about postcards. That they would know about safety pins. That they would know about felt pens. But you would be wrong.'

He curled round in a perfect circle, his paws over his nose.

'Postcards?'

'*Have* you any?' he yawned.

'There's a packet in the table drawer,' suggested Ragdolly Anna.

'So there is!' The Little Dressmaker drew it out, and counted the cards. 'Only three left!'

'Three,' went on the White Cat sleepily, 'is the correct number. All the best things come in threes. Think of the Three Bears . . . the Three Wise Men . . . a Three-cornered hat . . . and now, Three postcards.'

'What shall we do with them?'

'A *fan*,' explained the White Cat patiently, 'is made of a number of strips, pinned together. Are you with me? Interrupt, if I do not make myself clear.'

'Do go on,' said the Little Dressmaker hastily. 'But I think I am beginning to see what you mean. I shall need my scissors . . . and some felt pens . . . and a pin.'

'Excellent!' The White Cat composed himself once more, and drifted towards sleep. 'Cut each postcard,' he instructed drowsily, 'into three pieces . . . All the best things are divided into Three Parts. Think of a cat: Head, Tail, and Middle. See?'

'And then, fasten them all together with a pin?'

'Exactly so!'

Ragdolly Anna grew quite excited, as she watched the Little Dressmaker find her scissors, and cut the postcards into narrow strips. 'Three threes are nine,' she whispered.

It was true. There were nine thin bits of card. The Little Dressmaker shaped them carefully, so that they were a trifle wider at the top than at the bottom.

'Would you like to colour them, before I pin them together? Do you feel well enough?' she asked.

Ragdolly Anna sat up in bed with her shawl round her shoulders. She had to be careful not to get the colours on the sheets, so the Little Dressmaker gave her an old tray to put the cards on, and brought out a selection of coloured pens. Ragdolly Anna coloured each strip differently: with stripes, speckles, squares, curly bits, stars and daisies.

Then they laid them out to dry.

The fan wasn't quite a fan, yet; but it was nearly.

When the paint was dry, the Little Dressmaker pinned the bits of card together at the thin end, and gave them a sharp Flip Flop.

They sprang open.

Flip Flop.

They shut again.

Ragdolly Anna clapped her hands.

'It's a fan!' she cried. 'I've got a fan! I can fan myself!'

At first, it was rather difficult to hold the fan so that it would stay out properly and not suddenly fold up when she was not thinking about it; but after a bit of practice she soon got into the way of it. And it *was* a comfort. She didn't feel *quite* so hot, with a breeze blowing on her cheeks . . . even if it was only a small breeze.

While she fanned herself, the Little Dressmaker was busy spring cleaning. 'It's a good opportunity,' she explained. 'You can lie quietly, and watch me.'

She began by turning out her dressmaking chest. There were all sorts of bits and pieces in it – some of them had been there for so long that she had forgotten all about them. There were pieces of velvet and lengths of braids, rolls of netting, stiffening for petticoats, and squares of blanket which could easily be turned into shepherds' cloaks.

Ragdolly Anna fanned herself, and dozed, and watched . . .

When the Little Dressmaker got to the bottom

of the chest, and was just going to give it a good dusting and fold everything up and put it back, she held up a piece of fine blue silk.

'What's that?' asked Ragdolly Anna, dreamily.
'It's a Japanese kimono.'
She gave it a shake. As the silk unfolded, you could see a pattern of willow trees, a river with lilies on it, and a boat, and someone fishing.
'It was for a fancy-dress party. But the person who ordered it was taken ill, and couldn't go. She never came for it.'

43

'Put it on!' pleaded Ragdolly Anna.

But the Little Dressmaker wouldn't put on the kimono. 'I'm too knobbly, my dear,' she explained. 'But it would look lovely on Dummy, wouldn't it?'

'And with the fan in her hand,' added Ragdolly Anna excitedly.

'When you're better, we'll give Dummy a treat.'

It didn't take Ragdolly Anna very long to get over her chicken-pox. In a few days she was about again. Not outside, of course, because the wind was chilly, but at least she could play by the window, and see what was going on down below. And she could talk to Dummy.

The streets were beginning to look gay and pretty, for it was nearly Easter. The shops were full of Easter eggs, and bright spring dresses.

'We might try and make an Easter window ourselves,' suggested the Little Dressmaker – 'with Dummy's help?'

So they turned Dummy round so that she could be more easily seen from the street, and dressed her up in the Japanese kimono with the willow trees and lilies. They put a dark wig on her, too, with a pretend lily stuck in a haircomb. And the Japanese fan hung on a cord at her waist.

I think Dummy was really pleased about the fan. Now and again, Ragdolly shook it open – Flip Flop – and fanned her, gently. Then you could see all the colours, and the patterns, at the same time.

People on their way to the High Street stopped, and looked up.

'Only a very *good* dressmaker could arrange a window like that,' they told each other.

One by one, they came upstairs to the flat on the fifth floor, and asked for the Proprietor.

The White Cat let them in. He had learned how to work the lift; he stood on his hind legs and pressed the button with a number FIVE on it, but he would not stop at any of the other floors. Never.

'Let them walk up, if that's what they want,' he said, haughtily.

The Little Dressmaker gained a great many new customers. She was so busy during March that they almost forgot to cook the dinner. But they managed, somehow. Ragdolly Anna took the small hard bits out of the potatoes with a tiny knife; she never cut herself once. What do you think of that? And once they had potatoes, they knew that dinner was half-way there.

By Easter, they had saved up quite a lot of money.

Ragdolly Anna picked up the cocoa tin, and rattled it. It was really heavy. So on the day before the shops closed for the weekend, they went out together, all three of them, and bought a teapot with a marigold on it, to go with the Little Dressmaker's cup and saucer.

'All the best things go in threes,' the White Cat reminded them.

'HAPPY EASTER!'

Ragdolly Anna
Meets a Fox

*

Ragdolly Anna was quite pleased to be as tall as she was – but there were times when it would have been convenient to be a bit taller. On Sundays, for example, when she was drawing back the curtains in the morning and the Little Dressmaker was still asleep. Or when she was drying the plates and glasses on the draining-board after dinner.

'Just a *bit* taller would be nice,' she explained gently to the White Cat. 'Because then I could do more things.'

The White Cat drew himself up. When he was sitting upright, and making a long neck, he was exactly the same height as Ragdolly Anna: not an inch more, or less.

'It's the most convenient height to be,' he insisted huffily. 'And as for *doing* things . . . let *her* do them. She's a human being, isn't

47

she? That's what they're for.'

He looked severely out of the window. His ears twitched. Then he peered closely through the pane.

'There's that fox again. I told you! Living under the old church on the corner, he is. Disgraceful! Foxes in the city? It shouldn't be allowed.'

'They do come into towns, sometimes,' ventured Ragdolly Anna. 'They come after the left-overs in the dustbins. Someone told me.'

'There should *be* no left-overs,' snapped the White Cat. 'You should finish them up. Waste not, want not. I shouldn't have thought I'd have to tell you that. After all, you were born in a boot-box. Some people . . . they just don't know *anything*.'

Ragdolly Anna peeped over his shoulder, and caught a glimpse of a fox's brush disappearing down some steps. He was going under the church. He really was.

'I wish I could see where he lives,' she whispered, half aloud and half to herself.

'Go and find out, then.' The White Cat yawned, and moved delicately along to a more comfortable cushion. 'Do what you like. Don't bother me, that's all. I'm going to sleep.' And he immediately curled himself up into a blob, and slept.

It was Dummy who gave a sort of tremble. Or was it only the bead necklace she was wearing – the one that was made of glass diamonds, and came out of a Christmas cracker? Ragdolly Anna wasn't quite sure. She turned back to the window. Yes, the fox was coming out again. He paused at the top of the steps for a fraction of a second, and then trotted off.

'It's a Sunday,' murmured Ragdolly Anna. 'And not many people about. That's why.'

The Little Dressmaker was visiting a sick customer with a dish of egg custard. She would not be back for an hour. Why shouldn't she do a bit of exploring on her own? She could leave a note, in case the Little Dressmaker got home before her. Left to herself, she began to feel really grown-up.

There was an old envelope in the waste-paper basket. Ragdolly Anna smoothed it out. The inside was clean. GONE . . . she wrote carefully, in large, clear writing. Then she bit the end of the pencil and sucked it for a minute. EX-PLORING, she added – first with two R's, then with one. One looked best. She reached up on tip-toe and put the note under an empty milk bottle on the draining-board. Then she pulled

her hat firmly over her ears, and whispered 'Goodbye!' to Dummy.

Eager, she hurried off. She thought she heard a rustle just as she was going out of the door, and for a moment she wondered if Dummy were coming too. Then she remembered Dummy had no legs. She only went out on special occasions, and needed a lot of help. Her shawl had slipped from her shoulders – I think she must have been twitching with excitement – and Ragdolly Anna ran back and rearranged it.

'I'm going to find out where Mr Fox lives!' she confided. Dummy shivered. She didn't think she wanted to know about foxes. They were mischievous animals. Mice were bad enough . . . they ran up your petticoats, and were inclined to tickle. But foxes! What would *they* do? She couldn't guess.

Out in the street, Ragdolly Anna glanced up

and waved. Then she walked on, trying to look as if she knew where she was going. Of course, with adventures, you never *did* know. Your feet took you . . . to the oddest places . . . especially if it were Sunday. The pavement was empty, except for a person or two hurrying along with a hymn book. Ragdolly Anna kept her eyes well open. She looked especially closely at gateways, houses with nobody in them, and places where builders had been at work: anywhere likely to provide a hidey-hole for a fox. She made her way carefully round drains, because she had once fallen down one and experienced the greatest difficulties in getting out again. And it was while she was counting her steps from one house to the next, and being sure not to trip on a kerb, that she noticed a dark and mysterious gap under the church wall.

'Just like a cave!' Ragdolly Anna exclaimed.

She put her head down, and peeped inside. There was certainly a strong smell of fox. And, at the end of what appeared to be a passage-way, shone two greenish-yellow lights.

'That's a strange place for traffic lights! I wonder where it leads?' thought Ragdolly Anna. It was a nuisance that the brim of her hat was rather wider than the opening, but by bending it a little at the sides she managed to

get her head through, and then it was easy for the rest of her to follow.

The passage was dark, and *very* stuffy. It went on and on.

'I hope I shall be able to find my way back again,' she thought. 'I ought to have dropped some pebbles, or breadcrumbs, behind me. Like Hansel and Gretel. That is what the White Cat would say. And why do the greenish-yellow lights keep moving? I'll never catch up with them, at this rate.'

She walked a little faster, but the walls of the passage grazed her elbows as she went. There wasn't much room. Perhaps it was a good thing she *wasn't* much taller, after all. And then, quite suddenly, the greenish-yellow lights grew larger ... a nose stuck out between them ... and two pointed ears just above.

It was Mr Fox.

Ragdolly Anna jumped. She hadn't expected to find him so soon; and she felt a little nervous. After all, she *was* trespassing. It was lucky she had her hat on, with the roses. That always made her feel brave.

'Good morning!' said Ragdolly Anna.

'What?' snapped Mr Fox sharply. '*Good* morning, did you say, Miss? What's good about it, I'd like to know? Not a single chicken bone to be had.'

'Chicken bone?' questioned Ragdolly Anna.

'Drumstick, wing or wishbone, I'm not particular,' went on Mr Fox in a wheedling tone. He looked at her sideways, in a way she didn't much like. 'Just a morsel for a poor old fellow's Sunday dinner, don't you know?' He rubbed his nose with his paw, and sniffed.

'Haven't you anything in the larder?'

'Nothing at all. Not a crumb. Not a sausage.' He licked his lips. 'I wouldn't say no to a ham

sandwich . . . or a steak and kidney pie . . . or turkey. A nice bit of turkey. That'd be tasty, that would! I suppose you haven't brought a snack with you?'

'I'm afraid not,' said Ragdolly Anna. 'How do you usually get your dinner? Do you buy it in a shop? Do you *steal* it?' (Perhaps I shouldn't have asked him, she thought a minute after-wards. It might not be polite!)

'Those as ask no questions will be told no lies. But since you've arrived without knocking . . . *and* with a hat on . . . perhaps you're the new kitchen maid?'

Mr Fox came a step nearer. Then another step. He really was uncomfortably close. 'The kitchen's first on your left,' he went on. 'In there. Apron's on the hook. Washing-up's in the sink. There's quite a lot – I haven't done any this week. Get a move on, will you? Then you might like to make a bread pudding. Out of crusts. There's crusts under the gas stove . . .'

'I'm *not* a kitchen maid, at all,' explained Ragdolly Anna, stepping sideways. But it was no use trying to get away. In a moment, Mr Fox had pushed her through the doorway, fastened the lock behind her, and slipped the key into his waistcoat pocket. It was a very dirty key, and there were lumps of suet stuck to the handle. I wonder if it had come out of a Christmas dinner? Even his waistcoat had marks of gravy down the front.

Ragdolly Anna was caught.

'It's silly to be frightened,' she said to herself. 'After all, he's only a fox.'

'And the finest fox in the county,' boasted her jailer. 'Mind you wash up properly, or you'll be in the pot before you know where you are!'

There *was* a big pot hanging over the stove, to be sure, and Ragdolly Anna could see that there was nothing in it except water, and a few feathers. She stood still for a moment, and counted up to ten. The White Cat had often advised this.

'Ideas are sometimes shy,' he had told her. 'I have plenty, mind you; but not everybody has. If you count up to ten when you are feeling fuddled, an idea will come while you are counting. See? That's how it's done.'

And it was perfectly true. She could feel an idea, perfectly close, by the time she got to eight . . . and when nine and ten were finished it came into her head as clear as a newspaper. The first thing to do was to trick Mr Fox. She thought she *could* . . .

'Very well. I'll get on with the washing-up,' agreed Ragdolly Anna, 'if you cover your eyes until I've finished. It'll be a surprise, see? A game.'

'That's a funny idea. A game, eh? Like Christmas? Like Blind Man's Buff? Only this once, mind. I'll put my brush over my eyes. That'll do. But get a move on. There's plenty to get on with. There's the beds to make and the floors to scrub, and a great deal beside.'

He turned his face to the wall, and held his brush over his eyes. It was a very thick brush . . . ENORMOUS . . . and he was proud of it. He couldn't see a thing.

Ragdolly Anna started to wash up. There *was* a lot of it, and no mistake. Plates and cups and knives and spoons and frying-pans and mugs and saucepans and dishes . . . all smeared with grease and gravy and cocoa and tomato soup. Such a muddle. When she had cleaned a dozen plates, she began to put her plan into action. It was best to be bold.

'I might as well wash the key, too, while I'm about it,' she remarked casually. 'It could do with a scrub. Just pass it over, will you please? Keys are important. A good polish will make it look like gold.'

'It *is* gold,' said Mr Fox, crossly. 'I should know. I stole it.' He fidgeted around in his waistcoat pocket. It was difficult to find things with his brush over his eyes, but he got it at last, after a lot of fumbling, and handed it over . . .

Trembling, Ragdolly Anna closed her fingers over the key. She had got it! How to use it and get away without being discovered – that was the problem! Holding her breath, she tip-toed to the door. It took only a second to fit the key into the lock. A quick turn – and she was away!

Only just in time. Mr Fox heard something that sounded suspicious . . . and opened his eyes with a start. Then, with a yelp of fury, he bounded after her.

Down the dark passages they scampered, whisking round the corners as quickly as the North Wind. Ragdolly Anna hadn't guessed she could get along so fast. Now and again she bumped her head on the ceilings, for they were rather low. Twice, her hat was bent and scratched at the edges. And, just before she reached the front opening, one of her shoes came off. She dared not stop to pick it up.

She could feel Mr Fox's breath only a few yards behind her when, with a final bound, she jumped out of the gap in the kerbstone and on to the pavement.

At that very moment, the church service had ended. People were coming down the path, holding their hymn books and chattering to each other.

Mr Fox took one look, and turned back to his den.

She was safe!

When human beings are walking together they don't notice such things as a rag dolly with only one shoe, and a hat all battered and bent at the edges. Ragdolly Anna was anxious to get home. She was out of breath, and dishevelled, as she ran up all five flights of stairs and burst into the living-room on the fifth floor.

'Where *have* you been?' asked the Little

Dressmaker. 'I read your message, but you've been such a long time. I was getting anxious.'

'I wasn't,' said the White Cat. 'Not everybody can be punctual. Some are. Some aren't. Remember that.'

'I've had terrible adventures!' broke out Ragdolly Anna. She began to tell her story. Dummy's eyes grew larger and larger as she listened. When the story got to the part where Mr Fox was hiding his eyes, she would have given a little cry, but although her lips opened slightly I don't think a sound came out. And when she heard how Mr Fox had chased Ragdolly Anna through the dark passages under the church, poor Dummy turned quite pale and had to be revived. The White Cat fanned her, slowly, with a table napkin.

'It's all a part of First Aid,' he explained loftily. 'One should know about such things. And foxes are undesirable,' he went on. 'Nasty, low creatures, not to be trusted. I myself would have nothing to do with them.'

The Little Dressmaker was stitching another shoe. She pursed her lips and nodded. Foxes were not to be trusted, that was certain.

Ragdolly Anna sat on the window seat, waiting for her new shoe, and thinking about her adventures.

'I shall put some odds and ends by the dust-
bin, now and then,' she decided. 'After all, he
was hungry. It must be hard for foxes to find
enough to eat in the city.'

The White Cat turned, and stared at her.

'*What* did you say?' he questioned haughtily.
'Odds and ends? *What* odds and ends?'

Ragdolly Anna smoothed her handkerchief.
'Perhaps a bit of bread pudding,' she murmured,
so softly that nobody else could hear. 'Foxes like
bread pudding. I know they do.'

At that, I think Dummy raised her eyebrows,
just the tiniest bit, and there was the suggestion
of an almost-smile.

New Bread
and Birthdays

*

The Little Dressmaker was making bread.

It wasn't often that she allowed herself such a treat. New bread, warm and sweet, straight out of the oven, was delicious; but it took a long time to prepare, and she was usually too busy with her sewing for such goings-on. But it was January Bank Holiday. The shops were closed and they had only two slices of bread left . . .

'Can I help?' asked Ragdolly Anna.

'You can help knead the dough,' answered the Little Dressmaker briskly. 'We'll use my best bowl.'

She drew a large enamel basin from the sink cupboard. There were roses painted on the bottom of it, and a red squiggly pattern round the edge. She put yeast, and sugar, and a little warm water in the bowl. Soon, the yeast began to wriggle and swell. Bubbles appeared on the

surface, and plopped . . . and new ones came. They measured the flour, and poured the yeast mixture into the middle of it. They punched and kneaded and pulled and stretched the dough, for ten minutes by the clock. Then they pressed it into a baking tin, covered it with a cloth, and left it to rise.

'Rise you shall
and rise you must,
soft in centre,
crisp in crust,'

chanted the Little Dressmaker. She lit the oven,

63

and heated it, ready for the bread mixture to go in when it was large enough.

The White Cat observed these activities with interest.

'Bread,' he announced, yawning, 'is the Staff of Life. That's what they say. Mind, they're not always right. I prefer sardines, myself; but then, I am an aristocrat, and have always been accustomed to the best. Has anyone remembered it is my birthday?'

'Your *birthday*?' Ragdolly Anna was surprised. She had never imagined the White Cat would have a birthday at all. But that was silly. Everything had a birthday – even the kitchen table. 'It must have been born,' she told herself, 'when the carpenter nailed the legs on, and it stopped being a tree.'

But the White Cat . . . where had *he* been found? And when? She didn't like to enquire.

'I was born,' explained the White Cat to anyone who happened to be listening, 'in a snowstorm. That is why I am so white. Ask *her*. She knows.' He nodded in the direction of the Little Dressmaker.

'It's true,' she admitted, 'he *did* arrive in the middle of winter. I found him curled up on some straw in a cardboard box, behind the Supermarket. Oh, it was cold! He didn't belong to anybody. So I took him home. I put a post-card in the window saying FOUND: A WHITE KITTEN – but no one paid any attention. So he stayed. I remember it was snowing at the time. Perhaps he *was* born on the January Bank Holiday? That's today.'

There was a faint sound from the window, where Dummy stood with an evening cape pinned round her shoulders, and a string of beads at her throat.

'Today...' she nearly whispered. 'Today...?'

By the time the bread was done, the loaf had been tapped, and turned upside down to cool, they began to realize that the White Cat was expecting something special.

'A birthday,' he mewed, 'is a Special Day. Everybody knows that. Something should be organized. In a well-governed household, it would have been organized *long* ago. Fortunately, the Houses of Parliament have re-membered. That is why we are having a Bank Holiday. There may be processions, later. I de-serve them. But we do not always get what we deserve.'

He twitched his nose, and stalked off to his favourite resting place in the airing cupboard. 'I leave it to you,' he threw over his shoulder. 'Whatever you think best. And if a telegram arrives from the Palace, send my regards to the Queen. And to the Duke of Edinburgh. Thanks.'

Ragdolly Anna and the Little Dressmaker looked at one another. It was quite clear that *something* had to be done; but the shops were closed. They couldn't buy him a present. They couldn't have a party, because it was too late to send out invitations. And there was no cake.

It wasn't much of a birthday, certainly.

The Little Dressmaker wore her anxious face – the one which showed a great many crinkles over the forehead, and at the corners of the eyes.

Dummy gazed into the room with her almost-smile, and both eyebrows slightly raised. She would have liked a party, I think, because she enjoyed dressing up – even if she seldom ate anything, for fear of spoiling her delicately formed mouth.

Ragdolly Anna took off her hat, rearranged the roses, and put it on again. It was funny, but the hat often helped her to think. It seemed to make her more human, somehow.

'I know,' she called out. 'I've got an idea. We'll have a miniature party: a miniature tea-table, and paper people!'

'Paper people?' The Little Dressmaker looked puzzled.

'*You* know. Like you showed me. I can make them myself,' said Ragdolly Anna.

She could, too. Once, when she had been in the big armchair with a rug and a tummy-ache, the Little Dressmaker had shown her how to fold a piece of paper over and over and over and over, and then how to cut shapes in it with her old nail-scissors. When the paper was unfolded, there had been a beautiful lace mat. Ragdolly Anna had made a set of mats. Then, she had learned how to fold a piece of paper over and over and over and over, and draw a person on the top side. She had cut out the person, going carefully through all the layers of paper, and *especially* carefully round the arms and legs. When it was unfolded, there was a long chain of paper people holding hands.

The White Cat had admired the mats, and the paper people. He had tapped them gently with his paw.

'I'll make a mat, for the table,' explained Ragdolly Anna, 'and twelve paper people for guests. If he sleeps until tea-time, he won't know anything about it. It will be a birthday surprise.'

Luckily, there was a pile of old paper in the larder, waiting to be sent somewhere. She set to work.

The centre mat was an immediate success. It came out like a sky full of stars and moons, and was most decorative. They put it on the table, and began to cut out the people. The people were more complicated. Their necks and shoulders and wrists and ankles had to be attended to with some skill, or they tore; and Ragdolly Anna was obliged to make several attempts before she managed to achieve twelve faultless paper people, all holding hands. True, the last had only one leg, but it did not matter.

They called him Wunny.

The paper people sat round the mat. They found it hard to sit up by themselves, but when Ragdolly Anna folded them in the middle with a crease, the result was splendid. Wunny was allowed to lie down.

'He feels happier, at parties, lying down,' explained Ragdolly Anna. She made Wunny a pillow out of a bit of cotton wool, and he lay down straight and stiff with both eyes open. He liked to watch what was going on.

When all was ready, they put the new, crusty loaf in the middle of the lace mat.

That smelt appetizing.

It wasn't everybody who had new bread for tea, and the paper guests appeared pleased, and grateful. Their table manners were excellent.

The Little Dressmaker laid the best china saucer for the White Cat: the one with flowers on it, and a gold rim. Luckily, there was a tin of sardines in the cupboard. She had a terrible job opening it, because the key got stuck, but at last the lid rolled back far enough to get the sardines out. There were four of them. Two were mashed up, because of difficulties with the key, but two were *perfect*, and they arranged them tastefully on a plate next to the milk.

They only just finished in time.

There was a faint, dull thump from the airing cupboard, as if someone had just jumped out of a nest of pillows and bath towels. A pause, as if that person were stretching himself. And then the White Cat appeared very slowly, bit by bit, arching himself round the edge of the door, and bringing his tail in last.

'Wow!' he ejaculated, when he saw the birthday table. 'A party, eh? A little celebration? A bit of jollity? That's just as it should be. I was expecting something of the kind. Thank you. Where shall *I* sit? Here?'

He settled himself by the two perfect sardines, and started to eat. A rumbling sound came from somewhere in his throat, but it didn't seem to interfere with swallowing.

The end of his tail twitched.

Ragdolly Anna and the Little Dressmaker spread the mushy sardines on their new bread. They saved a tiny, tiny crumb for each of the paper people; and for Wunny, there was a raisin, too, which had been lying on the bottom of the gas stove since Christmas.

You might have thought that was enough. But just as they were finishing, they heard the noise of drum-beats and trumpets. To begin with, it sounded as if it were a long way off. Then it grew closer and closer, and louder and louder; and when they rushed to the window to look out, far below – like toy soldiers – they could see the Boys Brigade, having their Bank Holiday Procession. The leader looked up, and saluted, as they went by, and twirled his drumsticks. I think the salute was for Dummy, because, standing by the sill with the evening cape round her shoulders, and beads, she really looked like royalty.

But the White Cat wrinkled his nose, and started to clean his whiskers.

'It's *my* procession,' he exclaimed loftily. 'For me. For my birthday. Of course.'

Nobody contradicted him. After all, it *was* a special occasion, wasn't it? And one should not have to suffer contradiction on one's birthday.

The paper people stayed on the table until after supper. Then, at last, they were cleared away out of sight.

Ragdolly Anna lay awake for a long time, after she went to bed that night. When she thought the Little Dressmaker must be asleep, she crept out, very very quietly, one step at a time.

She reached the drawer where the mats and table napkins were kept. She put in her hand, and felt around, fumbling, in the darkness.

She brought Wunny out of the drawer, and

folded him up carefully inside her pocket handkerchief. Then she nipped back into bed again.

She tucked Wunny carefully under her pillow.
It was cosy and safe there, you see. I think he
liked it. A person needs a bit of looking after, if
he is cut out of paper and has only one leg.

And after all, it was *his* birthday, too. Wasn't
it?

Ragdolly Anna
Goes on Holiday

*

The Little Dressmaker was mending sheets. Some of them were old – so old that they had her grandmother's name inked in the corner. They had holes in them, now, and she carefully cut out the empty places and turned the sheets sides to middle. The mended sheets were a bit smaller . . . One or two were so small they would do for a baby's cot, or even for Ragdolly Anna's bed. But they wouldn't be wasted.

When she was just finishing off, the White Cat stalked in, looking important.

'Busy?' he enquired. 'Some people are too busy to notice *anything*.'

'Notice what?' asked Ragdolly Anna. She had made up her bed freshly with a proper little sheet, and was proud of it.

'I suppose you know it's raining?'

'I *did* know,' said Ragdolly Anna. 'I

could smell it. It's got a special smell, rain.'

'We could hear it, too,' added the Little
Dressmaker. 'Such a noise! Aren't we lucky, to
have a dry place to live in?'

'That's exactly the trouble,' explained the
White Cat. 'It's *not* dry. There's a tile off. The
roof's leaking. And there's a patch on the ceiling.
If I'm not mistaken, it's getting bigger.'

He wasn't mistaken – he never was. There
was a brown patch over the table with curly
legs. At first, it was only about as big as an
eggcup, but it grew larger and larger as they

stood looking up, and drops of water gathered at the edges. Plip . . . plop . . .

'It would be sensible to move the table,' went on the White Cat, 'before things get worse. It would be *COMMON* sensible to put a bucket underneath to catch the drips. But then, not everyone *HAS* common sense. Only me, I sometimes think. Is milk being served?'

The Little Dressmaker opened a new bottle and poured an inch or two of cream into a saucer. He always liked cream, and soon there was a deep, rumbling sound as if someone were purring. By the time the rain had finished they had collected quite a lot of water in their bucket.

'We'll wash our hair,' decided the Little Dressmaker. 'Rainwater's good for rinsing.'

So they did, and when it was dry again their hair seemed especially shiny – but the White Cat showed no interest. He was sitting up, straight and stiff, and called Ragdolly Anna to come and make a list for him.

'A list of *what*?'

'A list of OBJECTS IN NEED OF REPAIR,' he explained, sternly. 'It's my opinion we shan't be able to live in this flat, five floors up, much longer. Not unless something is *done*.'

'Not *live* in it? What's wrong?'

'For one thing, the heating isn't working properly. I found myself a little chilly in the airing cupboard this morning. We need a new hot-water tank and central heating through-out.'

Ragdolly Anna wrote down: HOT-WATER TANK AND CENTRAL HEATING THROUGH-OUT, and waited, with her pencil in her hand, for the next thing.

'A new ROOF,' he went on.

That was easy to spell, but it sounded rather expensive.

'Railings to be repaired.'

'Railings?'

'The railings on the outside staircase,' he added impatiently. 'There are several missing. You might fall over – it's dangerous. Not to me, mind. I wouldn't fall. I never do. But *you* might. And then what would happen?'

'I would have to go to Hospital,' whispered Ragdolly Anna.

'New sink . . . new drainpipes . . . new taps . . . new window-sills . . . new electric wiring . . .' went on the White Cat, rapidly.

She wrote and wrote. When he had finished, they counted, and there were twenty-seven things wrong with the flat five floors up, that needed mending.

'Add to *THAT*,' mewed the White Cat, 'it's on the Council Books to attend to it. My friend Professor Purrkins told me. He saw it written down. No doubt a letter will come. We shall see.'

And the very next morning, a letter *did* come. It was in a long, special sort of envelope, so that it wasn't a bill – because Ragdolly Anna knew bills nearly always were sent in brown ones that had windows to them. It was printed, and told them that the roof was to be repaired, and the ceilings, too ... and several other things. It would be a messy job. They would have to move out for a few weeks, and find somewhere else to live, taking their best bits of furniture with them so that it wouldn't get spoiled. Quickly, too, for the lorries would arrive quite soon, and men would begin taking the tiles off.

At once, they began searching for rooms.

'It's no good looking at what we can't afford,' decided the Little Dressmaker. 'We want a place quite small . . . and simple . . . and not too noisy. Just to keep us going. Oh dear, I have a feeling it's going to be difficult.'

'I am prepared to offer my assistance,' said the White Cat, graciously. 'Professor Purrkins and I will make a survey of the neighbourhood.'

'A survey?' questioned Ragdolly Anna.

'He means they'll look around,' explained the Little Dressmaker. 'We'll *all* look.'

She had stopped feeling sad. It would be quite an adventure.

They dressed themselves up warmly, explained to Dummy where they were going, and set out . . . They walked and they walked and they walked. By dinner-time they were nearly worn out, but there were still several more flats to look at. They had a bun and a sandwich quickly, and rested a few minutes, and then they went on.

'Twenty-seven floors up is *not* where I would like to be,' settled the Little Dressmaker firmly. They had gone up in the lift, and when Ragdolly Anna peeped out of the window she felt slightly dizzy. Were those *real* people, so far below? They seemed no bigger than thimbles . . .

The next flat was over a fish-and-chip shop, and they found the White Cat and Professor Purrkins inspecting it already.

'Just what we need,' mewed the White Cat. 'A continual supply of fish on the premises. What better?'

But the Little Dressmaker thought her sewing might be scented with frying oil, and that she would lose her customers in consequence. Another advertisement offered three rooms quite near to a tube station. They liked the place, and had almost taken it because it was on the ground floor and there was a lamp post outside. But a tube train came by just as they were making up their minds, and there was such a roaring and a shaking that they could not hear one another speak, and Ragdolly Anna thought it would be like living in the middle of a volcano. So *that* was of no use, either; and by the time evening came and they were making their way up the rickety outside staircase – being careful to keep close to the wall in case of loose railings – they had found nothing.

'Whatever can we do?' sighed the Little Dressmaker. They were eating baked beans and drinking cocoa, for they were too exhausted to prepare anything else. Ragdolly Anna's hat was rather limp. She gave it a little shake, and put it on more firmly. Not everybody wears a hat with roses on while they are having their supper; but then, not everybody has got one.

'You'll think of something,' she said comfortingly. 'Don't worry!'

'She may be able to worry – but she can't *think* much,' drawled the White Cat. 'Anybody who does not want to live over a fried fish shop must be *ill*; in need of helpful, nourishing food, and good conversation. If the decision were mine, I would take it.'

It was just when they were wondering whether it would matter if a figured satin wedding gown were scented with frying oil, that the Little Dressmaker had an idea. To begin with, the idea was quite small. It grew, and grew, and grew. Even Dummy, who had been covered with a dust sheet all day, began to tremble.

'I know!' the Little Dressmaker cried suddenly, breaking into a smile. 'We'll go and stay with my brother. My brother Ted. The one who was a sailor. Can you remember him, Ragdolly Anna? You saw him just before he set off on his last voyage. He's retired, now, and turned into a lock-keeper. A lock-keeper, on the canal!'

'What does he live in?' asked Ragdolly Anna. She could remember Uncle Ted very well. He was a bit like Bob the Bargee to look at, but his eyes were paler – such a pale, pale blue they looked as if they had picked up a bit of sea water and were always staring into the distant horizon. He walked in a rolling way; he still felt the deck of a ship under him – even if he were on dry land . . . even if he were at the Recreation Ground or the allotment.

'I'll write at once,' decided the Little Dressmaker, 'and ask him what he thinks.'

As soon as they had cleared the table, she wrote – not in her usual slow, careful hand, but quickly, for she was excited. 'Have you any spare rooms?' she queried. 'And could you put up the four of us? There'd be Ragdolly Anna – but she doesn't take up much space; and the White Cat . . . and Dummy . . . and me.'

Then she paused. The lock-keeper's house was right next to the canal. It had a lawn . . . and flower beds. 'We'd be very pleased to come,' she finished enthusiastically. Then she sealed the envelope, and the White Cat took it to the post immediately.

Two days later came a postcard. There was a picture of a steamer on one side of it. 'Come at once. All are welcome. Ship ahoy! Make for the harbour!' it said on the other, and was signed: 'Your loving brother, Ted'.

I think that Dummy caught a little of the excitement that followed, for Ragdolly Anna told me – years later – that there had been a faint squeak . . . exactly as if there were mice around. And they knew that there weren't.

Then the busy time began. Not *all* the furniture in the flat belonged to the Little Dressmaker. Some could be left behind. But the table with curly legs was hers . . . and the sewing machine . . . and their beds. They collected cardboard boxes from the grocer, and put all their clothes into one marked EVAPORATED MILK; they wrapped the china up gently in bits of newspaper, and stacked it in SLICED PEACHES IN HEAVYSYRUP. They took down the curtains and washed them and wrapped them up.

At last, everything was ready.

But what were they to do for a van? Removals were expensive. The lock-keeper's house was only just past the outskirts of the town; a few miles from the flat five floors up. Bob the Bargee had a horse – and a barge, too. The White Cat suggested that this would not be large enough, but that another light, empty barge could be roped on to the first, and it would be convenient and comfortable for them all to travel by water. He, and Professor Purrkins, would Make

Arrangements . . . they would fix time and place
. . . for the barge horse was an old friend, and
they were certain he would be helpful. Horse,
his name was.

So that's what happened.

The day of Removal shone clear and bright.
Several journeys by wheelbarrow took all the
smaller things to the canal where they were to
embark. Only the table with curly legs proved
difficult, but Bob the Bargee said a chum of his
who drove a brewer's dray would bring it. And
he did!

Could it be possible, thought the Little Dressmaker, that nothing would go wrong?

It was the White Cat who suggested they
might have a last look round.

There, still covered with a dust sheet in the
empty flat five floors up, stood Dummy, hidden
behind a pile of rubbish and an old sofa which
didn't belong to anyone. She had a spider's web
on her chin, and had lost her smile altogether
– there might even have been a tear trickling
down her cheek. I am not sure. But nobody likes
to be forgotten. They kissed her, and hugged
her, put her straight and carried her downstairs.
She had travelled in the wheelbarrow before, so
that sort of thing wasn't frightening at all – but
the two barges roped together were a great sight!

They placed Dummy in the prow, which is what the front of a ship is called, and wound a warm scarf round her neck, and laid two shawls across her shoulders so that she should not catch cold. She wore a sailor's hat, too, which they had found. Anyone could see she was the Captain.

The old horse gave a tug and a pull . . . the ropes strained . . . and they were off.

What a journey it was! Horse took his time. He wasn't one for hurrying. The barges moved slowly and calmly, leaving a faint ripple behind them. On the banks of the canal, factories and warehouses turned into hotels . . . then into houses . . . then into a cottage or two. They passed fields with cows in them, and a collie dog rounding up sheep. At last – after what seemed like a whole day but was really only an hour and twenty minutes – they drew up in a channel before two enormous wooden gates: gates which held back the water, and had to be opened, slowly, to let the barges through.

'It's the lock!' cried the Little Dressmaker joyfully. 'There's the house . . . isn't it pretty? And there's Uncle Ted! We've arrived!'

What a welcome they had! 'Ahoy, there! Throw us a rope, and drop anchor!' It was easy to guess that Uncle Ted had been a sailor: they

were hitched up, helped ashore, and unloaded in no time. And while the Little Dressmaker and Ragdolly Anna, and the White Cat and Bob the Bargee, were given tea in the kitchen, and big, new currant buns, Dummy stood at the window and looked out, her almost-smile breaking a little at the edges, and an expression of delight in her eyes.

The lock-keeper's house seemed to have only one storey to it. 'It's a bungalow!' cried the Little Dressmaker. 'No stairs!' But Uncle Ted explained that there was a tiny flight of stairs hidden away behind a door where you would least expect to find them, and these led up to a bedroom under the roof, where he slept himself. He took them up, to see. Ragdolly Anna thought it was a lovely room, for the ceiling was slanted and rose to a point in the middle, and there were windows all round. You could see fields out of one . . . and a little garden with rosemary and sweet williams out of another . . . and out of the biggest – the canal itself, and the barges coming and going, into town and out again.

'I sit there, in that armchair,' explained Uncle Ted, 'and watch for the boats, see? Then I go down, and work the lock. Not much goes by in winter, but come the summer I'm hard at it till dusk. I could do with a bit of help. You'll soon learn the way of things. We'll have to make sailors of you. Ahoy, there! Your horse is eating my roses! We'd better give him his rum!'

So they went down, and gave Horse some carrots and apple, and a bit of bread, since he said he did not fancy rum. Then they stood by the door and watched the barges move off.

'Goodbye!' they called to Bob the Bargee. 'And thank you!'

'Ta-ta!' he called back. 'So long! Thanks for the buns! I couldn't have made better myself!'

By that time Horse had pulled his load slowly round the bend of the canal, and they could see them no longer. 'So long . . .!' came faintly on the air . . . and then, nothing.

Ragdolly Anna gave a little skip.

'It's going to be exciting, living here,' she said to the White Cat softly. 'Things will happen! What do *you* think? They'll happen, won't they?'

'Of course they will!' answered the White Cat. 'They always do. Whether one is here, or there . . . coming or going . . . still or active. It makes no difference. Mind you, the fishing will be good! We'll have to see about that . . . But now is the moment for sleeping. I am off to find the airing cupboard. If there *is* one.

Good-night!'

Other books by Jean Kenward

RAGDOLLY ANNA

Although she's only made from a morsel of this and a tatter of that, Ragdolly Anna is a very special doll. And within hours of beginning to live with the Little Dressmaker, the White Cat and Dummy, she embarks on some hair-raising adventures.

THREE CHEERS FOR RAGDOLLY ANNA

Six more exciting adventures for Ragdolly Anna. She is trusted to do all sorts of things for the Little Dressmaker, but somehow nothing ever seems to go right. Her balcony garden turns into a jungle, a misguided stranger hands her into a lost property office, and she's nearly bought as a fairy for a Christmas tree!

DINNER AT ALBERTA'S
Russell Hoban

Arthur the crocodile has very bad table manners, until he is
invited to dinner at Alberta's.

MARGARET AND TAYLOR
Kevin Henkes

Seven simple stories featuring Margaret and Taylor, a brother
and sister whose competitive relationship leads to lots of
amusing and instantly familiar domestic incidents.

THE ELEPHANT PARTY AND OTHER STORIES
Paul Biegel

A circus elephant gives a wonderful party, a witch's shoe
punishes a cheeky boy, and lots more in these 11 enchanting
stories, both funny and fantastical.

ON THE NIGHT WATCH
Hannah Cole

At the end of term the classrooms and playground will be locked and never used again. But no one is happy with the idea of sending all the children to different schools, and so teachers, parents and pupils get together to draw attention to their cause, all determined to keep their school open. Can the council be persuaded to change its mind? There is a very effective way of forcing them to listen . . .

THE THREE AND MANY WISHES OF JASON REID
Hazel Hutchins

Eleven-year-old Jason is a very good thinker. So when Quicksilver (no more than eighteen inches high) grants him three wishes, he's extremely wary. After all, in fairy tales, this kind of thing always leads to disaster. So Jason is absolutely determined to get *his* wishes right. But it's not that easy, and he lands himself and his friends in all sorts of terrible but funny scrapes!

MR BERRY'S ICE-CREAM PARLOUR
Jennifer Zabel

It is thrilling enough to have a lodger in the house – after all, not even Andrew Brimblecombe has a lodger – but Carl is over the moon when he discovers that Mr Berry plans to open an ice-cream parlour.